# This igloo book belongs to:

........................................................................

# igloobooks

*Published in 2019*
*by Igloo Books Ltd, Cottage Farm, Sywell, NN6 0BJ*
*www.igloobooks.com*

*Copyright © 2018 Igloo Books Ltd*
*Igloo Books is an imprint of Bonnier Books UK*

*1019 002.01*
*2 4 6 8 10 9 7 5 3*
*ISBN 978-1-78905-190-2*

*Written by Melanie Joyce*
*Illustrated by Gabi Murphy*

*Designed by Hannah George*
*Edited by Hannah Campling*

*Printed and manufactured in China*

# Snuggle Up Tight

igloobooks

It's the end of the day.
No more play, toys away.

Stars out, moon out, too. Bedtime for you.

Up the stairs to run the taps on the bath. Bubbles. Boats.

# Gloop - shloop.

Rocket pyjamas,
nice and clean.

Brush your teeth
until they gleam.

Hop into bed.
Snuggle, cuddle.

Time for a story, the one
about the fairy? Nothing scary.

Sssh, settle down now.
Goodnight, sleep tight.

Click goes the light.

It's quiet and still.
Until...

... **Whooo!  Tap-tap.**

What's that?
A cat, a bat?

Is someone outside? Quick, hide.

Don't look. Don't peek.
Try to go back to sleep.

Then, **tappety-tap!**
There it is again.

Squeeze Ted tight. It's scary at night.

Squeeze Bunny, too.

# Hoo-hoo!

Peek outside.

Eyes wide.

Who's there?
A tap. Then another.

Throw back the cover.

# Rattle
# tap-tap

on the window.

Time to go!

Run across
the floor.

Dive for the door.

There, there, let's go and see.
We'll find out what it could be.

It's not a monster,
just a tree, see?

**Whooo!**
goes the wind.

It blows the branches
to and fro.

So they
**tap-tap-tap**
on your window.

# Hoo-hoo!

It's just an owl, in the night.

Snuggle, cuddle. There are no monsters,
or scary sounds. No shadows moving around.

Time to snuggle up tight.
Goodnight.